Mrs Holmes-Seedley's Musical Cats

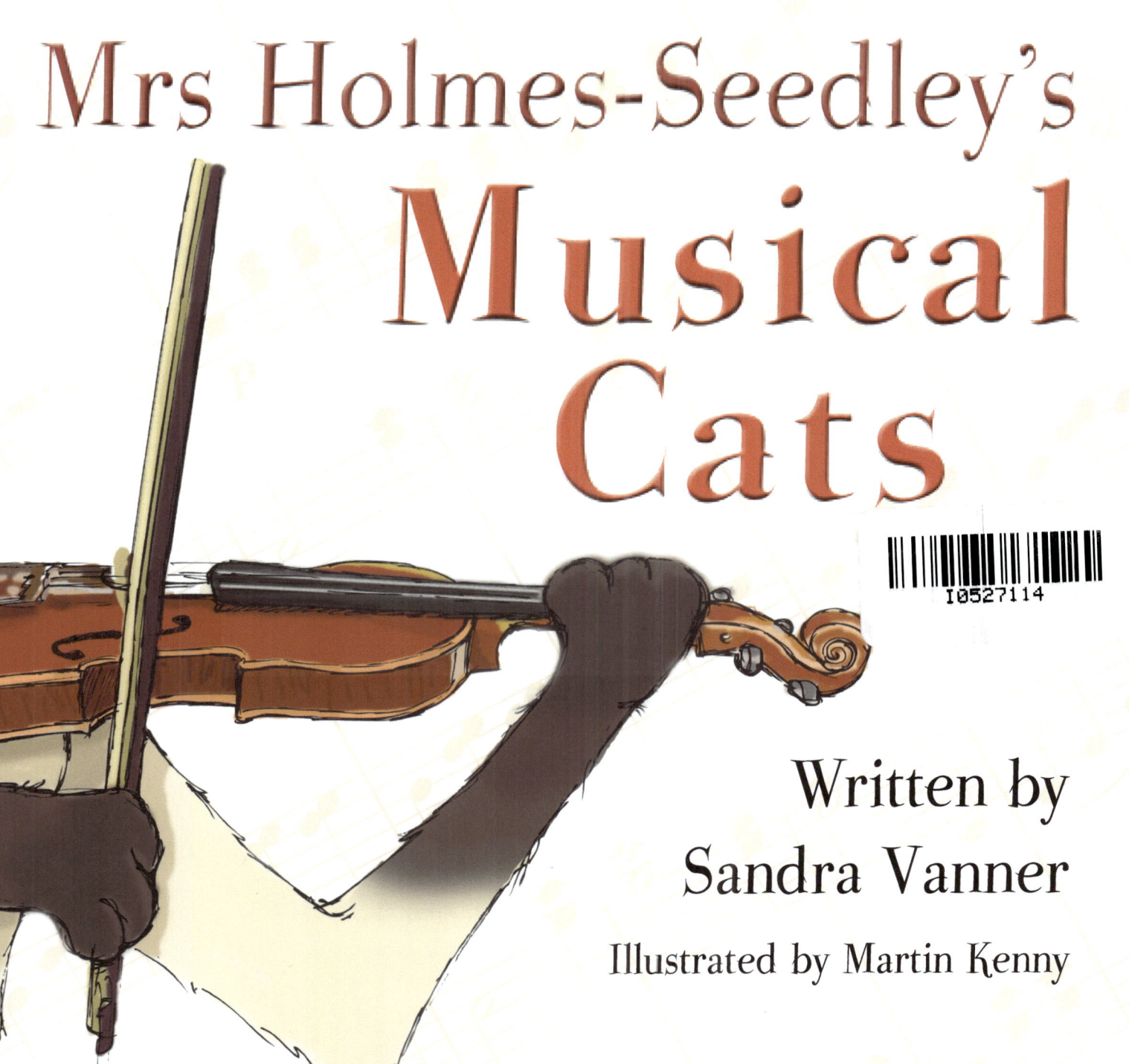

Written by
Sandra Vanner

Illustrated by Martin Kenny

I0527114

Published by New Generation Publishing in 2012

Copyright © Sandra Vanner 2012

First Edition

www.newgeneration-publishing.com

New Generation Publishing

Mrs Holmes-Seedley's
Musical
Cats

Written by

Sandra Vanner

Illustrated by Martin Kenny

Mrs Holmes-Seedley was rather an eccentric woman; which really means she was considered a bit odd! She was a retired music teacher, wore very brightly coloured clothes, and lived in a large ramshackle house with her 6 cats. These consisted of 2 Siamese, 2 Persian and 2 Burmese, and she named them, Beethoven, Chopin, Debussy, Mozart, Greig and Liszt.

No-one would need to know a lot about music to understand that these 6 cats were all named after famous musicians!

Mrs. Holmes-Seedley had taught these 6 cats to play various instruments and they were exceptionally talented. Naturally, her neighbours were pleasant enough and paid no attention, when at practice mornings her very grand voice was heard calling out to her cats, 'Enough, Enough Beethoven, you are playing it far too fast!' or 'Really Debussy, do not keep teasing Mozart, that sort of behaviour is very unbecoming and will not do at all!'

The Rector, Canon Winri a very good man who had known Mrs Holmes-Seedley for a long, long time received a visit from Mrs Holmes-Seedley one bright spring morning. He welcomed her warmly, asked after her many felines and when she ventured to inquire as to how the funds for the new roof for the church were progressing, was told that it was coming along, but very slowly!

Mrs. Holmes-Seedley said, 'Yes, I thought as much myself, which is why I requested to see you,' adding 'I think I have a plan that might just assist in raising some money towards the re-roofing project.'

Canon Winri was very touched by this and said, 'That is most kind of you Mrs. Holmes-Seedley,' and smiling at her said, 'What had you mind?

'Well Rector,' she said, 'I know that I am thought to be an odd sort of a woman, and I expect maybe I am; however, you are aware that I have cats, but I think you have never actually heard them.'

'Oh!' replied the Rector, 'Yes, I understand they are,' he paused, 'somewhat musical'.

'Yes, indeed,' she replied adding, 'We have been practicing a lot of late and it occurred to me that if I were to give a concert, assuming of course,' she added, 'that you would allow me to use the large hall, we could charge the public a small entrance fee, to be entertained by my musical cats, and of course,' she beamed, 'It is all for such a worthy cause.'

The Rector smiled and said that while he thought it an excellent idea, inquired when she planned to hold the concert, explaining that the large hall she mentioned is always in great demand for various activities.

'I would have to check and see
what dates are available,' he told her.

'Well,' responded Mrs Holmes-Seedley,
'I can accept that and I hope Rector
you will not think it forward of me to
say that my musical cats are exceptional and I
expect not only you, but indeed the majority of the
community will be presently surprised at their talents.'

Later that evening, the Rector called into the large hall
mentioned as he knew that on Tuesday evenings, the
hall was used by the lady members of the 'Flower
Club'. None of these ladies were surprised
to see their Rector in their midst and after
looking at some of the lovely arrangements,
he asked Mrs. Cotts, who was
responsible for organizing various
events in the large hall,

'I wonder, Mrs. Cotts, if you would be able to find out for me whether or not the hall would be free on,' here he paused and took out a small diary from his pocket, 'Oh! one evening in June say?'

Mrs. Cotts who knew just about everything that went on in the parish, as well as her duty insofar as the booking of the big hall was concerned, furrowed her brow slightly and replied 'Well, Rector, from memory, I think there is only one Friday left in June; let me get my book,' she added, and delved into her large handbag sitting on a nearby chair.

The rector waited patiently glancing at the floral arrangements, so beautifully presented in various vases and urns; their bright colours; their scent filling the old hall with a lovely aroma.

Mrs. Cotts said, 'Now, I was right; the only date it is free in June is the last Friday.' She looked up at him and added, 'What exactly is the hall needed for?'

The Rector, rather reluctantly told her of Mrs. Holmes-Seedley's proposition, whereby, she looked quite astounded and said, 'Oh, Indeed.'

She added that of course the various bodies who used the large hall would need to be consulted.

The Rector understood this perfectly, but asked if she would pencil the date in.

The word of course flew round the parish very rapidly. People were generally amused by the prospect of a concert and since they all knew Mrs. Holmes-Seedley and had heard of her musical cats, feelings were rather mixed. Some thought it an excellent idea, others pooh-poohed the very idea of being entertained by cats who professed to be musical!

In the meantime, Mrs. Holmes-Seedley continued practicing with her 6 musical cats. It was the middle of May and since the concert had been arranged for the last Friday in June, it meant she only had about 6 weeks to prepare her programme.

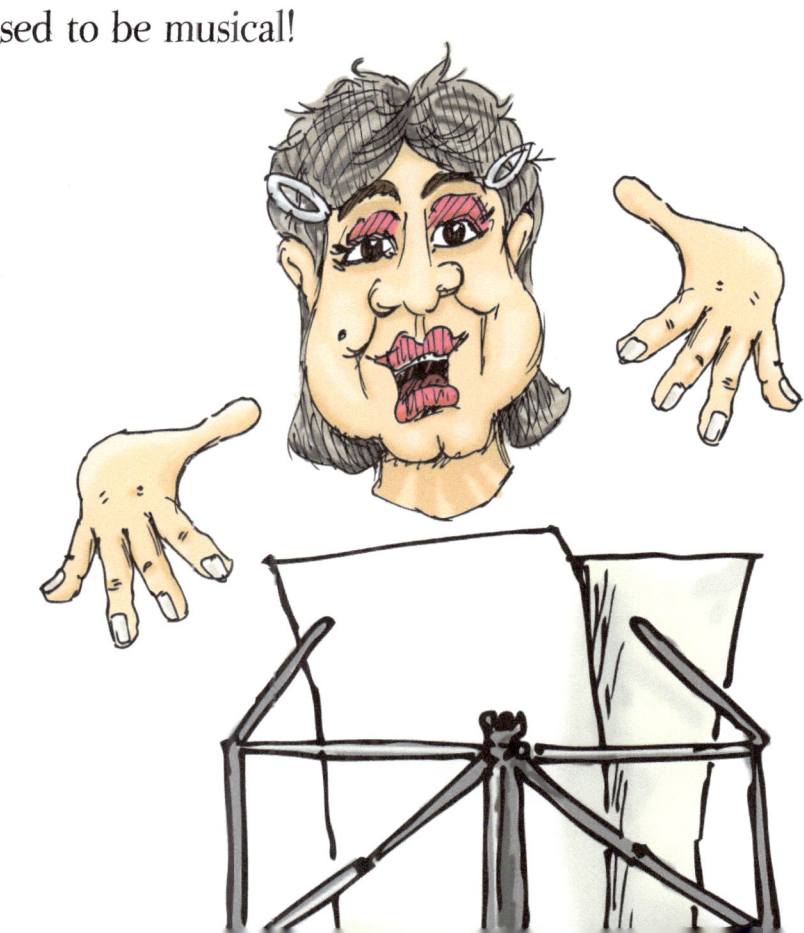

Those who lived in the neighbourhood heard the playing of piano pieces; the sounds wafted up and down the quiet street and many ladies hanging out washing or working in their gardens, wondered who was playing such pleasant music. No-one would have believed for a moment it was being played by 6 cats!

The Rector called one morning at Mrs Holmes-Seedley's house, and was very surprised as he stood at the front door, to be greeted by what he definitely knew was Beethoven's Moonlight Sonata! He knew of course that Mrs. Holmes-Seedley herself played the piano, but when she opened the door

and he could still hear the music, he was temporarily unable to say anything but, 'Ah, Mrs. Holmes-Seedley, glad I found you in.'

She was of course delighted to see him and took him into her music room. Here again, the Rector was rather stunned! A large and magnificent blue Persian was sitting at the piano playing that tune he had recognized. On the large sofa, a beautiful Siamese, and another Persian sat listening to the pianist! Another Siamese was sitting on the windowsill, and two Burmese were sleeping on the back of the other chair! The room was littered with sheets of music, a harp was sitting in the centre of the room; a cello too was observed and several clarinets and two violins.

When the music had ceased, Mrs. Holmes-Seedley, clapped her hands with delight and was joined by the Rector, as she exclaimed, 'Well, done Mozart, Magnificent, magnificent!!'

'You'll take a cup of tea, Rector?' she asked.

The Rector was viewing the entire menagerie with a look of amazement. 'What? Oh, I beg your pardon, Yes, a cup of tea would be very nice.' he uttered.

He noticed that the blue Persian, who had been sitting up playing the piano, now lay relaxing on the seat as if nothing out of the ordinary had happened!

Mrs. Holmes-Seedlie returned with a small tray and after offering the Rector a seat began to pour the tea.

'What did you think? she asked him, handing him a cup and saucer.

'I am, Mrs. Holmes-Seedley,' said the Rector, 'at a loss for words.

MRS DRUCILLA HOLMES-SEEDLEY
AND HER MUSICAL CATS
PRESENTS

AN EVENING OF MUSIC

TO BE HELD ON JUNE 28ᵀᴴ
AT 7:00 P.M.
IN SUPPORT OF OUR NEW ROOFING PROJECT
PLEASE COME ALONG,
EVERYONE WELCOME

I daresay had I not seen and heard, I would have been incredulous!'

'Oh!' she said, her large smile spreading over her broad face, 'I am so pleased you called.' 'You know Rector, I think the element of surprise is a good tactic. I am well aware of the scepticism of some members of the community, and that of course does not trouble me, but I think it will turn out to be a marvellous concert!'

'I have had tickets printed up, you know,' she said, and produced a cardboard box on the floor beside her chair. She selected a ticket from this and presented it to the Rector. 'I have set the price at £5.00 per ticket; I hope you do not think that too much!'

He looked at the ticket and read:

MRS DRUCILLA HOLMES-SEEDLEY
AND HER MUSICAL CATS
PRESENTS

AN EVENING OF MUSIC

TO BE HELD ON JUNE 28TH

AT 7:00 P.M.

IN SUPPORT OF OUR NEW ROOFING PROJECT

PLEASE COME ALONG,

EVERYONE WELCOME

The Rector said, 'I think this is admirable, Mrs. Holmes-Seedley, well done!'

While he sipped his tea, Mrs. Holmes-Seedley made him known to the other cats.

Starting with the blue Persian whom the Rector had already witnessed playing the piano, she called out 'Come here, if you please, Mozart,' and the cat ambled towards her and sat down on the floor.

'This,' she said, directing her gaze at this lovely Persian, 'is Canon Winri. He has, of course, heard you play and is very impressed.' The cat fixed his amber eyes on the Rector and gave a soft meow!

'Now, run along and send Beethoven to me,' she urged.

A tall Siamese made his way to Mrs. Holmes-Seedley's feet and she introduced him to the Rector, explaining that like his namesake, he too suffered from acute deafness, but while it made him sometimes a bit cross, he coped with it admirably.

Another Siamese, Greig, another Persian, Chopin, and two Burmese were brought forward, Liszt and Debussy.

He asked Mrs. Holmes-Seedley if they all played the piano or looking round the music room, did some of them play other instruments.

'Oh! Yes,' she replied, 'All of them are very versatile and can play the other instruments. Greig, she pointed to a Siamese, is particularly fond of the violin and plays delightfully.'

The Rector was then briefly entertained by each one of these felines.

Debussy played a short piece on the harp; Litsz played the piano.

Chopin also played the piano,
Greig played the violin, Beethoven the piano.

He said to Mrs. Holmes-Seedley
before taking his leave of her, 'I
think this is marvellous,' adding
'What patience you must have, it is
certainly wonderful and will, I am
sure, convince the worst sceptics.'

Later over tea, the Rector related to
his wife what had happened during his
visit that day to Mrs Holmes-Seedley.
She was as surprised as he was but said,
'Well,' I can believe it. You know, dear,
Mrs. Holmes-Seedley may be a little
eccentric, but she is extremely talented
herself and I am not surprised that her
cats have had the benefit of her experience.

I think it is terrific. I predict, after what you have told me and possibly, after the concert, she will be much in demand and we are liable to see her on the television; hear her on the radio and her picture and that of her cats gazing out at us from the local newspapers! '

The evening of the concert arrived. It was a warm June evening and Mrs. Holmes-Seedley dressed in a long black evening skirt, sprinkled with sequins; her bright long red silk blouse was finished with a large red belt around her ample waist. She wore green shoes with yellow bows which just peeped out beneath the folds of the long skirt! Her hair was clipped back with very shiny hair slides and the vision she presented

caused many in the huge audience to raise their eyebrows and smile, but in a kindly way!

All the tickets had been sold and the large hall filled up very quickly!

Mrs. Holmes-Seedley had herself arranged the transport of her various instruments to the hall and had spent a good part of the afternoon, kindly assisted by several stout men, putting all in place.

Her 6 musical cats were brought along later and when the Rector took to the stage to announce the commencement of the concert and declared the venue open;

when the curtain rose, Mrs. Holmes-Seedley stood on the stage in all her finery and each of her cats, attired in different coloured jackets with a matching bow-tie surrounded her.

She turned to the audience and said, 'My Blue Persian, Mozart, will start us off.

'Mozart, if you please.'

Mozart took his seat at the piano; Mrs. Holmes-Seedley raised her baton and he began to play. As the stirring notes filled the hall, looking around,

the Rector found everybody's eyes fixed on the cat at the piano and a few open mouths as the paws of this feline flew up and down the keyboard.

When Mozart had finished; there was a stunned silence, but suddenly hands were together, and the ringing applause brought a dazzling smile to the face of Mrs. Holmes-Seedley!

She brought Mozart forward to more applause and he bowed very gracefully towards the audience.

'Next,' she said, ' We will hear my Siamese, Greig; 'He will play the violin.'

This sleek chocolate coloured cat took to the stage and tucking the violin under his chin began. Sometimes the violin, if playing a very sombre piece, sounds as if it weeping, but Greig, played several jaunty little folk tunes, causing the younger members of the audience to clap their hands, and feet as the jovial notes, played so superbly, so lightly filled the room.   It was smiling music! There was no hesitation of hands joining in applause when he had finished!

Beethoven was introduced next. He too was a Siamese and he played the piano. He had great presence, lifting his beige coloured paws up from the piano, throwing himself into the music; as he played a lively little Russian dance tune. Again, the audience applauded and since everybody was evidently much surprised and some astounded at this extraordinary concert, the eagerness on the faces, the smiles, the nods to each other observed closely by Mrs. Holmes-Seedley, swelled her heart to near bursting!

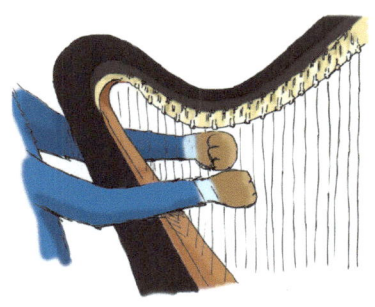

Chopin, another Persian, played the Harp. Mrs. Holmes-Seedley loved the harp and Chopin plucked the strings, so gently, so finely, as the beautiful Lieberstraume echoed around the hall. You could have heard a pin drop as he came to the end.

This time, the audience took to their feet, cheers of 'Bravo,' 'Bravo,' started and Chopin, strolling over to stand beside Mrs. Holmes-Seedley was very, very pleased. Mrs. Holmes-Seedley was almost overcome!

When the hall was silent, Mrs. Holmes-Seedley announced, 'And now, my two Burmese, Lizst, on the piano, and Debussy on the harp will play a lovely duet for you.

Once again, silence reigned and the hushed audience listened in awe at the incredible talents of these two cats. To look at, it was almost impossible to tell them apart, except that Dubussy,

as Mrs. Holmes-Seedley knew, was very temperamental, he had of course a lot of French blood, but he behaved beautifully and refrained from a lot of head-tossing and grandiose gestures which he was very prone to enact! At the end, rapturous applause.

She brought them both forward as the applause continued and the audience certainly by now knew which of the cats was Debussy, for he bowed and waved and smiled with such grace and finesse that Mrs. Holmes-Seedley could not possibly have scolded him!

'Finally,' Mrs. Holmes-Seedley announced, 'We will end our programme with all of the cats playing together and I am sure there is no need for me to tell you that this tune is familiar to all of us; it is Strauss' Blue Danube Waltz!'

Each of the cats took their places and as the strains of this beautiful waltz began, Mrs. Holmes-Seedley surprised the Rector by inviting him to waltz with her, which he did and pretty soon, others in the audience joined in and the big hall was turned into a scene of gaiety with everybody joining in and enjoying the music.

'There never was anything like it' could be heard as the concert came to an end to thundering applause!

The proceeds of the concert tickets and those who paid at the door accumulated a huge amount of money which Mrs. Holmes-Seedley presented to the Rector who thanked her profusely.

As predicted by the Rector's wife, Mrs. Holmes-Seedley was indeed solicited by the press, radio and television but declined all publicity stating that neither herself or her musical cats would entertain such vulgarity!

Since that wonderful concert, the only small problem which has arisen is that the organist is now overwhelmed by persons wanting to join the choir, who prior to the concert, showed no interest in music at all! He told the Rector that there simply was not the space for such numbers.

After hearing this, however, the Rector's wife said, 'Well I think there is no need for concern,' adding,

'You know, should the numbers swell that much, with the help of Mrs. Holmes-Seedley and her musical cats, who knows, we probably could raise enough money to build a cathedral!!'

'Oh Yes,' replied the Rector, a vision of a large cathedral with a magnificent spire flitting across his mind, 'Oh, Yes, indeed.'

- the end -

These two books were also written by Sandra Vanner. They are alive with colour and should bring a smile to young and old alike.

This well-mannered visitor with a love of bannana cream pie made a big impression on dad as well as the garden.

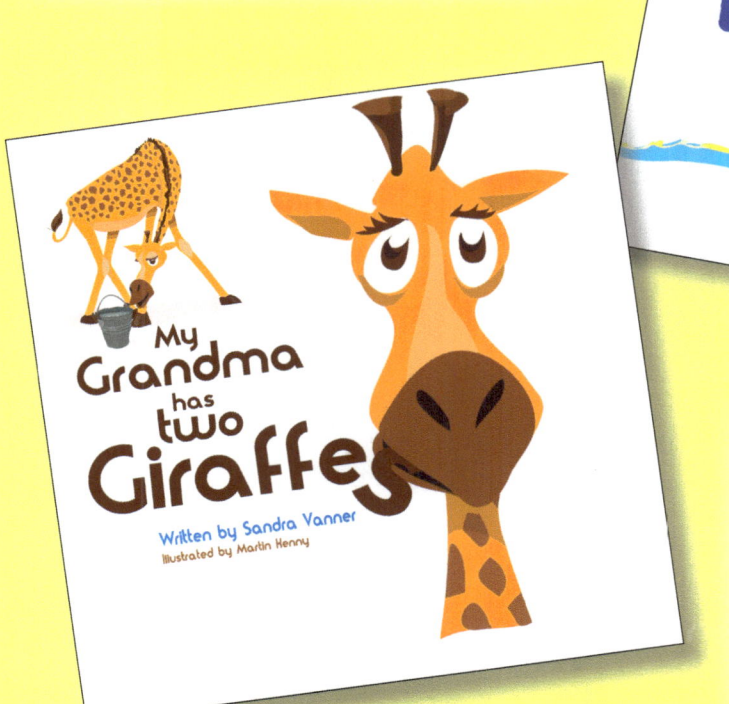

GEORGE AND THE DINOSAUR
By Sandra Vanner
Illustrated by Martin Kenny

My Grandma has two Giraffes
Written by Sandra Vanner
Illustrated by Martin Kenny

Was grandma telling fibs or did she really have two giraffes in her back garden? Maybe it was a dream?

About the author

Sandra lives in Lisburn Northern Ireland along with her husband John. They have two sons who have grown into fine young men. Although reading is her favourite past-time, she also enjoys gardening, playing piano, cooking and listening to classical music.

She was born at Ballymacash, Lisburn, the seventh child of a family of ten (five girls and five boys). Sandra attended both Ballymacash and William Foote Primary School where she was encouraged to develop her natural ability in self-expression particularly through writing.

At home there was a wealth of literature at her disposal. Her mother regularly took time to read to her thus reinforcing the value of a well written book. With such a large family it could get noisy at times yet it remained a happy home. Whatever was lacking in material luxuries was more than made up for in love, laughter and encouragement.

Lisburn Technical College is where she acquired the skills of a secretary including the very useful ability of writing in shorthand. Sandra went on to live and work in America for a time before she returned home and was married in 1970.

While her two boys were growing up she worked in temporary jobs. Payments received for her short stories from publishers helped supplement her income and fuel her passion for writing.

Sandra believes that the beauty and magic of the written word can be enjoyed by young and old alike. When imaginations are stirred up books can be every bit as exciting as any modern toy.

www.ingramcontent.com/pod-product-compliance
Lightning Source LLC
Chambersburg PA
CBHW041546240626

47164CB00003B/143